THE NETHER ATTACK

THE NETHER ATTACK

AN UNOFFICIAL LEAGUE OF GRIEFERS ADVENTURE, #5

Winter Morgan

Sky Pony Press
New York

Sky Pony Press books may be purchased in bulk at special discounts for
sales promotion, corporate gifts, fund-raising, or educational purposes.
Special editions can also be created to specifications. For details, contact
the Special Sales Department, Sky Pony Press, 307 West 36th Street, 11th
Floor, New York, NY 10018 or info@skyhorsepublishing.com.

Sky Pony® is a registered trademark of Skyhorse Publishing, Inc.®, a
Delaware corporation.

Minecraft® is a registered trademark of Notch Development AB.
The Minecraft game is copyright © Mojang AB.

Visit our website at www.skyponypress.com.

10 9 8 7 6 5 4 3 2 1

Library of Congress Cataloging-in-Publication Data is available on file.

Cover photo credit Megan Miller

Print ISBN: 978-1-63450-539-0
Ebook ISBN: 978-1-63450-954-1

Printed in Canada

TABLE OF CONTENTS

THE NETHER ATTACK

1
A TREASURE HUNT

Violet and Noah were talking to their friends Trent and Will, who were visiting the town. They were filled with new stories about their latest treasure-hunting adventure beneath the ocean.

"Tell us about the elder guardian!" Violet was always happy to hear about the duo's adventures. She often day-dreamed about going on a treasure hunt.

"The elder guardian is scary. He has a large eye that follows you." Trent's eyes opened wide as he talked about the menacing fish.

Will added, "The eye can see you at all times. Even if you use the potion of invisibility, the elder guardian's eye can still see you."

"Wow! How did you escape?" asked Noah.

"It wasn't easy. At one point I was struck by its laser and got Mining Fatigue," admitted Trent.

"I was pierced by the elder guardian's thorns." Will shuddered as he said those words. The memory of the elder guardian's attack was still fresh in his mind.

"Why do you put yourself in those types of situations?" asked Noah. "It sounds very dangerous."

"It's also a lot of fun!" replied Trent.

"And we finally found the treasure room in the ocean monument," said Will.

"Really? What did you find?" asked Violet.

Will was excited to tell them about the loot they had discovered. "We found a room filled with gold bars."

"Gold is very valuable," remarked Noah.

"The best part is when we got to the shore and found an abandoned mine. We went mining and discovered twenty diamonds!" exclaimed Will.

"What are you going to do with all of those diamonds?" asked Noah.

"We don't have that many," confessed Trent. "We had to share them. We were on the treasure hunt with our friends Henry, Max, and Lucy."

"Where are they now?" asked Violet.

"They went to visit their friend Steve who lives on a wheat farm. They're taking a break from treasure hunting."

"Taking a break?" Violet said aloud. "So, you have nobody to join you on your next trip?"

"Trent and I were just planning to go together. We usually meet people on the way," replied Will.

Violet wasn't looking for any trouble when she suggested, "Maybe Noah and I could go with you on your next adventure."

"Really?" Will was shocked, but thrilled. "That would be fantastic!"

Noah looked at Violet. "But we can't leave our village. We need to keep a watch for Daniel and his band of evil rainbow griefers."

"Noah, we haven't been attacked by Daniel in ages. The last time he tried to attack us was at the grand opening of the amusement park, Supersonic. I think it's safe for us to leave town."

"I'm worried *because* Daniel hasn't attacked us in a long time. I suspect he must be staging something very large. This isn't a good time to leave." Noah didn't want to go on a treasure hunt. He wasn't a fan of exploring the Overworld. He'd rather stay in the village and help Violet with her building projects.

"Noah," said Violet, "we don't have to go on a long trip. We can take a quick one."

"I'd rather not," replied Noah.

"That's okay," Violet said. "I'll just go by myself with Trent and Will."

"Fantastic!" Will was excited that Violet was going to join them on their next adventure.

"We heard about a treasure in a Nether fortress," Trent told Violet as he glanced at Noah. "Do you want to help us search for the treasure?"

Suddenly, Violet began to have doubts. She remembered her last trip to the Nether. It was an ominous place with flying mobs that shot fireballs at her. "Umm, m-maybe," she stuttered.

Noah looked at Violet and noticed she seemed afraid.

Violet was surprised when Noah said, "Yes, we would. I think this would be a great adventure for us both."

Violet had to admit she was happy Noah was joining them. She was glad there would be four of them on this treasure hunt through the lava-filled landscape of the Nether.

"Great," Trent said. "I'm going to craft a portal."

"Right now?" Violet asked. She thought they'd have more time to prepare.

"Yes, I think we should leave as soon as we can. You never know who might be searching for the same treasure," Trent told them.

"But it's getting dark." Violet looked up at the sky. Night was approaching, and she wanted to head back to the tree house.

"There is no day or night in the Nether. This is the perfect time to travel there," said Will.

"Okay," Violet agreed, "but I think I should let Hannah and Ben know that Noah and I are leaving. They will be worried if they can't find us."

Noah added, "And we should ask them to keep a watch over the town. You never know when Daniel might attack us again."

"That's fine," said Trent. "We can build the portal in front of Hannah and Ben's house."

Noah suggested they head over there immediately. "We have to get there fast because it's getting dark and we don't want to battle hostile mobs. We need to save all of our energy for our trip to the Nether."

The gang walked toward Hannah and Ben's house. When they reached the yard, they saw Ben picking some carrots.

"Hi, I was just getting some food for breakfast," Ben said.

"Hey! We wanted you to know that we're going on a treasure hunt with Trent and Will." Violet was so excited that she spoke her sentence in one breath.

"How exciting!" Hannah called out. She was standing in the entrance to the house.

Ben assured them, "We'll keep an eye on the town while you're away."

"Yes, please watch out for Daniel," said Noah.

Suddenly the night grew darker and then Hannah screamed, "Ouch!"

An arrow struck her chest.

"Oh no!" Violet spotted a cluster of skeletons in the distance.

The gang put on their armor and took out their weapons. Noah shot an arrow at the skeletons.

"I'll make the portal while you battle the skeletons," Will said.

"But we can't leave Hannah and Ben to fight alone!" Violet was upset.

"She's right," Trent said, and he aimed his bow and arrow at the skeletons.

Two skeletons approached the house. Hannah threw a splash potion on them, instantly destroying the bony beasts.

Noah shot an arrow at a skeleton and obliterated it. "Only one more to destroy and then we've destroyed them all."

Ben defeated the final skeleton.

"Hannah and Ben should join us on the treasure hunt," Violet suggested.

"Let's do it!" Hannah said to Ben. "It sounds like fun."

"But who will watch over the town?" asked Ben.

"We won't be gone for too long," said Violet. "And the townspeople are strong. They're warriors, too."

Will crafted the portal. A purple mist permeated the air. Trent, Violet, Noah, Hannah, and Ben hopped onto the portal to begin their adventure in the Nether.

2
SKELETON ATTACK

The group emerged in the Nether. Within seconds of entering the red landscape, a ghast shot a fireball at them.

"Maybe this wasn't such a good idea," said Violet, as she dodged the flames.

Noah took a snowball out of his inventory and threw it at the ghast, obliterating the fiery beast.

"Do you know where the Nether fortress is located?" Noah asked Trent and Will.

"Yes, we were told it's near the epic lava waterfall," replied Will.

"Where's that?" asked Noah.

"It's . . . umm . . ." Will didn't have an answer.

"It's not too far away," said Trent.

"You guys don't know where it is, do you?" Violet was annoyed.

"We sort of have an idea of where it is." Trent looked at the netherrack ground.

"Let's not argue over this." Ben was ready for an adventure, and he knew getting lost could be fun, even if they were lost in the Nether.

"Watch out!" Hannah shouted as another white ghast flew through the air.

Again, Noah grabbed a snowball from his inventory and aimed for the ghast, striking it before the evil creature could fire at them.

"Good job," said Ben.

Violet looked at the lava stream that flowed past them. "Do you think this stream leads to a waterfall?" she asked.

"Let's follow it and see," replied Ben. The gang began to walk alongside the stream. They kept a close watch for ghasts and other hostile mobs that spawned in the Nether.

"Ouch!" Hannah was shocked when an arrow punctured her arm. "What is this?"

"It must be griefers!" Ben looked for Daniel's signature rainbow army, but there weren't any colorful creepers in sight.

"Oh no!" Hannah's mouth opened in surprise "How could this be?"

Just then, a horde of skeletons approached the gang. The aggravated skeletons shot arrows and a few struck Noah.

"I need some milk or a potion of healing," Noah requested. "I'm all out. Anyone have some? My health bar is diminishing."

Hannah offered Noah a potion of healing. "Take this," she said.

Noah drank it and thanked his friend. He then mustered up enough energy to shoot another arrow at a skeleton, destroying it.

Hannah dashed over to the skeleton's dropped bone and handed it to Noah.

Noah placed the bone in his inventory and asked the group, "Do you think the skeletons followed us through the portal?"

"I think you're right. They must have followed us. We have to break the portal!" Hannah screamed as a group of zombies lumbered toward them, behind the bony skeletons.

"This means we're going to have to battle the hostile mobs of the Nether *and* of the Overworld." Hannah's heart began to race as she spoke those words.

The gang went into overdrive while they battled the skeletons and zombies that were lurking in the Nether. Arrows flew through the air. Noah took out his enchanted diamond sword and, weaving his way through the group of skeletons, he rushed toward the zombies.

The zombies outnumbered the skeletons and both hostile mobs outnumbered the friends from the Overworld.

"How are we going to survive?" Violet questioned as she struck a skeleton.

"I don't know, but I think we may have some help." Hannah pointed at three creepers that lurked behind a crowd of skeletons.

"That's not help. They're creepers! They are harmful to us." Violet was perplexed at Hannah's reaction to the creepers.

The skeletons struck the creepers with their arrows and destroyed them. The creepers dropped gunpowder and discs.

"I want to grab one of those discs. They have great songs!" exclaimed Ben. He had always wanted a disc that was created when a skeleton destroyed a creeper, but Hannah warned him that it was too dangerous to collect it now. If he did pick one up, a skeleton could destroy him.

"Do you think Daniel tampered with the portal?" asked Violet.

"Is that even possible?" asked Hannah.

"How would Daniel know we were traveling to the Nether?" Ben wasn't convinced this was one of Daniel's schemes to destroy them. Maybe they weren't paying enough attention to who followed them through the portal. Also, when a portal is made in the middle of the night, there's always a possibility for hostile mobs to hitch a ride.

"Do you want me to break the portal?" Will asked his friends, as he shot arrows at the skeletons and zombies.

"Yes," Trent replied. He was worried more hostile mobs would emerge unless the portal was destroyed.

Will sprang into action. When he reached the portal, he attempted to break it but another hostile mob came after him.

"Help!" Will's voice was loud and shaky. He was very nervous.

"What's wrong?" Hannah asked, as she hurried to Will's side.

Two spider jockeys unleashed a flood of arrows at Will and Hannah. She had her answer. There was something wrong—something terribly wrong.

3
THE ONLY ESCAPE

As Hannah dodged arrows, Will struck the skeleton riding a black spider with menacing red eyes.

"We can't do this alone!" Will shouted.

"The others are too busy to help," Hannah said, as her arrow hit the skeleton and it was destroyed.

"Good job!" exclaimed Ben. "I'll get the spider. You fight the other spider jockey."

"You're giving me all the hard work," Hannah pointed out. She continued to battle the spider jockey, but it wasn't easy. Her health bar was diminishing rapidly.

Will destroyed the spider. "Don't worry, Hannah. I can help you."

"Great, but I see two Endermen walking in the distance," Hannah informed her friend as she struck another skeleton with an arrow.

"Don't stare at the Endermen!" warned Will.

"You don't have to tell me that." Hannah was annoyed. "I know it's foolish to stare at the Endermen."

Hannah and Will were weak, but they were still able to defeat the final spider jockey.

"We need to help the others now," Will said.

Hannah took a potion out of her inventory. "Take this first," she said and handed the potion to Will.

"Thanks," Will replied as he gulped it down.

Hannah sipped the potion too. As she placed it back in her inventory, an Enderman shrieked and teleported in front of her. Hannah was shocked and said in amazement, "I didn't even stare at the Enderman. This doesn't make sense."

"Run toward the lava," Will called to his friend.

Hannah listened to Will. She was worried that she'd slip into the lava, but she thought if she stopped before the pool of lava, she could push the Enderman into the pool. Hannah held her breath as she got close to the dangerous liquid. The Enderman didn't notice that Hannah halted moments before she reached the lava pool. He kept running and fell into the lava—and he was destroyed.

"Where are the other Endermen?" Hannah looked around, but couldn't spot the lanky block-carrying mob.

Will and Hannah heard cries in the distance.

"It sounds like our friends need help," said Will, and they ran toward the noise.

"We can't help them until we break the portal," Hannah reminded him.

Will raced over to the portal and smashed it with his fist, breaking the portal.

Their friends' cries grew louder.

"We have to help the others!" Ben took out his bow and arrow.

Hannah shot arrows at the zombies. There weren't many left, but in the meantime, more skeletons had spawned.

"We're losing energy," Violet called out breathlessly.

Hannah rushed to Violet's side and gave her a potion of healing. "I'm running low on this potion."

Violet took one of the last sips. "Thanks. Now what will we do?"

"We'll figure that out once we finish this battle," Hannah told her friend.

Once the skeletons and zombies were defeated, the group resumed their search for the Nether fortress.

"I think I see something!" Ben pointed at a structure in the distance.

The group used their last bit of energy to jog toward the structure. When they got closer, Noah called out, "It *is* a Nether fortress!"

As soon as they reached the entrance, three blazes shot fireballs at them.

Noah shot an arrow in retaliation. Violet threw a snowball. They all tried to dodge the cascade of fireballs, and finally the fireballs stopped.

"We did it!" Trent was happy they were able to defeat the blazes.

Hannah rushed inside the fortress in search of Nether wart for her potions.

"I found some!" She reached into a patch of soul sand and picked up the Nether wart.

"Watch out!" a voice called out.

Hannah looked up and saw a magma cube bounce inches from her leg. She grabbed her diamond sword and hit the cube, destroying it. She then realized the voice that had warned her about the cube wasn't a familiar one.

"Who are you?" she asked as she pointed her sword in the voice's direction.

"Don't hurt me!" a man wearing a black suit begged Hannah.

The gang entered the room and saw Hannah threatening a stranger with a sword.

"What's going on?" asked Will.

"This person is trying to destroy me!" cried the man in the black suit.

"Hannah, put the sword down," Trent told her. "We know him."

Hannah listened to Trent and placed the sword in her inventory.

"This is our friend Otto," Trent told the group. "Will and I used to treasure hunt with him."

"I've missed you guys," Otto said as he looked at Will and Trent.

But the reunion was cut short as three blazes shot more fireballs at the group.

"Snowballs!" Otto shouted and handed snowballs to the gang. The ice-cold balls of snow struck the fiery blazes and destroyed them.

"We got them!" declared Ben.

"No, we didn't. There are more coming." Otto pointed at three more blazes flying through the Nether fortress.

"I bet there's a spawner in this fortress," Trent warned, and he began to search the many rooms that filled the structure.

Will followed closely behind Trent as the others pelted the flying yellow beasts with snowballs.

"I see the spawner!" Trent called out.

"We need torches!" Will shouted.

Noah threw a snowball with one hand and grabbed a torch with the other. "Here you go. Let's deactivate this spawner."

Will and Trent destroyed the spawner, and the gang finished their battle with the evil blazes.

Once everything was calm, Violet suggested, "Let's go find the treasure."

Trent led the way through a long hall. Finally, he turned to the right. "This is where we usually find treasure."

Hannah stopped when she spotted mushrooms growing in a dimly lit area of the fortress. "Mushrooms! I want to pick these and place them in my inventory. They come in very handy when you're brewing potions."

Hannah started collecting the mushrooms while the others followed Trent. Once Hannah had finished picking up the mushrooms, she continued toward the treasure and found the group standing around three empty chests.

"Somebody has already taken the treasure." Will shook his head and stared at the empty chests.

"I wonder who took it?" pondered Ben.

A loud familiar voice boomed from the end of the hall. "I did!" the voice said with a sinister laugh.

4

SMALL MISTAKE, BIG PROBLEM

"**D**aniel!" Noah shouted.

"Yes, my old friend," Daniel laughed.

"We're not friends!" Noah shot an arrow at Daniel to confirm that fact.

Daniel sprinted out of the Nether fortress and the gang chased him. The group was surprised to see Daniel alone in the Nether. He usually traveled with his evil rainbow griefer army. Noah shot another arrow at Daniel and this time it pierced Daniel's leg and slowed him down.

"I think I got him, too," Violet called out as she charged up next to Daniel and struck him with her enchanted diamond sword.

Daniel fought back with his sword. He hit Violet, but he was outnumbered. The others began to attack Daniel. His health bar was very low. With one more hit, he would be destroyed. Just when the gang was about to defeat Daniel, two ghasts flew at them and shot fireballs in their direction.

Noah and Ben hit the ghasts with snowballs, and then saw that a horde of skeletons was marching toward them.

"Ouch!" Hannah cried as an arrow hit her leg.

The gang began to battle the bony beasts.

Click! Clack! Clang!

The skeleton army flooded the group with a sea of arrows. The gang was so distracted by fighting the skeleton invasion they didn't notice that Daniel had escaped.

"Where's Daniel?" asked Violet as she looked out onto the red landscape of the Nether.

"Did we destroy him?" asked Ben.

"Or did one of the hostile mobs do it?" wondered Hannah.

"No, I think he got away," Violet said. She was annoyed.

"There's no time to discuss it now. We are surrounded." Noah was fighting as many skeletons as he could hit.

"Oh no!" Trent pointed at the ghasts that flew toward them.

"This is an impossible battle!" cried Violet.

Click! Clack! Clang! More skeletons appeared in the distance.

"There's only one way out of here," declared Noah.

"What is it?" Hannah's voice quavered.

"We need to build a portal." Noah began to craft a portal as he dodged arrows that shot through the sky.

"This time when we build it, we must break it right away after we use it. We can't let any of the hostile mobs from the Nether enter the Overworld," said Trent.

"Wait!" Ben called out. "Maybe we should look for Daniel first?"

Two arrows struck Noah, and he looked at Ben and yelled, "Are you joking?"

A purple mist rose through the air. "Let's all get onto the portal," Violet said. They quickly made their way onto the portal and back to the Overworld.

When they arrived in the Overworld, the sun was shining, and cows were grazing peacefully in the meadow.

"Well, that was an adventure, wasn't it?" Hannah walked toward their village.

"It wasn't the fun adventure that I imagined," Violet said. She was disappointed.

"And we didn't find any treasure," remarked Trent.

"I know! Daniel stole all the treasure." Their new friend Otto was upset also.

"I wonder where Daniel is hiding," said Will. "Maybe we can find him and get the treasure back."

"That doesn't sound like a good idea. Unless Daniel is attacking us, I think we should leave him alone. Also, he found that treasure first. I hate to admit it, but that treasure belongs to Daniel." Even Noah couldn't believe he had spoken those words.

"I'm just glad it's sunny and we don't have to battle any more hostile mobs. I just want to go home to the tree house." Violet was exhausted. She regretted ever suggesting that they go on a treasure-hunting adventure, and she was glad her days of treasure hunting were over.

"Watch out!" Trent shouted.

"You spoke too soon, Violet." Otto grabbed a snowball from his inventory and hit the white ghast that flew toward them.

"We forgot to break the portal!" Will was shocked by their mistake.

Trent ran to the portal and slammed it with his fist, breaking it. But it was too late. Hostile mobs from the Nether were already invading the Overworld.

Four blazes shot fireballs and a group of magma cubes leaped toward the gang.

"This is awful," proclaimed Hannah, and she used every weapon in her inventory to battle the pesky mobs.

Just then, Valentino the Butcher approached the group. He reported, "The town is being attacked by flying monsters!"

Once Noah heard that information, he told his friends, "I don't think the portal was the problem. I think Daniel is behind this."

Hannah threw the last snowball at the final ghast, as Violet defeated the remaining magma cubes.

"We're ready to help!" Hannah told Valentino, and the gang hurried back to aid the townspeople.

On the way back to the village, Valentino told them about the invasion. "There are yellow and white flying creatures that breathe fire."

"Those are blazes and ghasts," Violet informed him.

"I don't care what they are called—they are destroying the village," Valentino continued, "and they've hurt so many villagers."

"How long has this been going on?" asked Noah.

"All night," replied Valentino.

Noah wondered if perhaps this was not Daniel's fault. Maybe the mobs from the Nether had slipped through the portal when the gang first entered the Nether on their treasure-hunting adventure. Noah wondered if this could have been their own fault.

As they reached the town, they saw flames and the damage the blazes and ghasts had inflicted on the homes and shops in the village.

Noah announced, "Everyone get out any snowballs that you have on hand. That's how you battle these mobs."

The townspeople grabbed snowballs and the gang began to battle the ghasts, blazes, and magma cubes.

"This is a nightmare!" shouted Hannah as a ghast shot a fireball at her. She tried to dodge the blast, but it hit her. Hannah was destroyed.

Violet threw a snowball at the ghast that incinerated Hannah. With one shot, Violet obliterated the fiery beast.

Violet was feeling confident that the townspeople would defeat the invaders, until she heard a familiar sinister laugh in the distance.

5

YOU DON'T BELONG HERE

The ghasts fired their blasts at the townspeople. The magma cubes pounced at the villagers. Thus began a terrible invasion as Daniel and his army of rainbow griefers marched into the town.

"You're the one who summoned the mobs from the Nether, aren't you?" Noah confronted the invader while he held his diamond sword against Daniel's chest.

Suddenly, the rainbow griefers shot a barrage of arrows at Noah, destroying him.

"Noah!" Violet shouted.

"Your friend is respawning somewhere." Daniel laughed. "And he'll never get to hear my response."

The rainbow griefers raced through the town, attacking anything that stood in their path. Daniel let out a loud laugh as he watched his army destroy the town.

"You might have a new army," Violet shouted at Daniel, "but you're not going to win!"

Daniel smiled and shot an arrow at Violet, destroying her.

Minutes later, Violet respawned in the tree house and called out, "Noah?"

"Violet, I'm here," Noah answered.

"I can't believe Daniel is behind this attack," she replied.

"It's better than the mobs creeping through the portal. Now we have a true enemy. And we know how to beat Daniel."

Violet sighed. "Well, I think we need to do a better job. Daniel seems to come back every time we destroy him."

"This time we will defeat him for good. Maybe we can place him on Hardcore mode."

Violet gasped. "Hardcore mode? Doesn't that seem extreme?"

"No, we need to end this reign of terror." Noah ate a carrot as he spoke. He offered one to Violet. They needed more energy for battle. As the two ate, Hannah and Ben ran up the stairs.

Ben demanded, "You need to help! The town is in ruins. There are fires everywhere. We have no idea what we're going to do!"

Hannah added, "We just respawned in our home. We could see the smoke rising from the center of the town."

The gang raced toward the town. Violet wanted to help, but she wasn't sure she was capable of solving this problem. She feared that Daniel had finally staged an attack they couldn't win.

"Do you guys have a plan?" Violet asked as they got closer to the smoking town.

Valentino the Butcher hurried past them. Noah shouted, "Valentino!"

The village butcher turned around. "I didn't see you guys. I was going to look for you. We need help. Something awful has happened."

"What?" asked Noah.

"Will was about defeat Daniel when Otto attacked Will! Your new friend Otto is apparently working with Daniel." Valentino could barely speak those words.

"I knew we shouldn't have trusted Otto," Violet remarked, although she knew it was a pointless comment. They *had* trusted him, and now they were in trouble.

"Did he destroy Will?" Noah was worried because Will would respawn in another village far from them. Will and Trent hadn't slept in the tree house recently.

"No, he isn't destroying them," Valentino explained.

"Then, what is he doing to them?" Violet was afraid to hear the answer to this question.

"Otto has a large bus. He placed Will and Trent on the bus and drove away using command blocks. I have no idea where he's taking them."

"Are Daniel and Otto gone?" asked Violet.

"Yes, but the flying flamethrowers are still here. There are so many mobs, and it's getting dark. If we don't destroy these flying terrors and cubes, our town will be destroyed by the morning," Valentino told them.

"But we need to find Will and Trent. Who knows what Daniel has planned for them? He could destroy them forever." Violet was worried about her friends.

"We will find them," Noah reassured her, "but we must battle these mobs first. Valentino is right—it's almost night, and we need to help the town."

Hannah added, "Also, we have no idea where Daniel has taken them. It could be anywhere in the Overworld. We might never find them."

Violet shuddered. "That's awful. How can you say that?"

Ben defended his friend Hannah. "She's right. Searching for Will and Trent might put us on a wild goose chase."

Violet was surprised at Ben's reaction. "But we can't just let them disappear. We must search for them."

"We will," Noah told her. "But let's concentrate on saving the town first."

The group walked toward the town. Fires were burning, and a ghast flew past Violet's head.

"Get out your snowballs!" Noah shouted.

The group pelted the flying terrors. Noah reached into his inventory and realized there were no more snowballs.

"Does anyone have a snowball?" he asked.

"I have one left," Violet said and, with a careful aim, she struck one of the ghasts and it was destroyed.

Hannah and Ben used their last snowballs to destroy the remaining ghasts and blazes until the sky was empty. As two magma cubes leaped at them, Violet struck one of the cubes with her sword, and it broke into two smaller cubes. Hannah annihilated the smaller cubes with her diamond sword. Violet watched as Noah and Ben defeated the other magma cube.

The townspeople emerged from their homes and applauded the group as they walked through the mob-free town.

Noah made an announcement: "We will defeat Daniel again. But we need to stockpile snowballs. Does anybody have snowballs in their inventory?"

There was silence. Finally one townsperson said, "We've used up all of our snowballs battling the Nether mobs."

Noah informed the crowd, "Until we find a way to stop the Nether mobs from spawning in our town, we need to gather snow. There is a cold biome just outside our village. We will travel there and make snowballs, but we need you all to keep a close watch on the town."

Someone in the crowd called out, "You can't leave! We need you to protect us!"

Another townsperson cried, "If you leave, the town will be destroyed!"

Noah reassured them all. "You will be fine. We will make a quick trip. Upon our return we will distribute snowballs to everyone in the village. If we don't have these snowballs, our town *will* be destroyed."

But the townspeople didn't agree with Noah. They still wanted the gang to stay and protect them.

Noah looked at the townspeople that crowded the center of the village. "I've watched you guys fight Daniel. Every one of you is a warrior. Some of you used to work for Daniel. Use that knowledge to beat Daniel at his own tricks. Be confident, and fight hard!"

With that speech, Noah and his friends began the hike to the icy cold biome. The sky was growing dark, and Violet questioned, "Do you think it's too dangerous to travel at night?"

"It's our only option. We are running low on snowballs. We need them to battle these mobs," Noah said quite confidently.

"Well, that's annoying. We can go search for snow, but we can't search for our friends," Violet complained.

"We will find Will and Trent. I promise," Noah said as he looked at Violet.

Violet hoped Noah would keep his promise. She knew she should be worried about the town's safety, but she couldn't stop thinking about her friends who were trapped on a bus taking them to an unknown part of the Overworld.

6

CLIMBING MOUNTAINS

iolet, Noah, Hannah, and Ben hiked through the grassy biome heading in the direction of the ice plains.

"Are you sure you know the way to the ice plains?" asked Violet.

Noah studied a map. They had stopped, as the night sky grew darker.

Hannah suggested, "Maybe Violet should build a structure for us to sleep in."

Noah studied the map a bit longer. "I think that might be a good idea."

"Yes, especially since I spot a group of zombies up ahead," commented Ben. He took out his bow and arrow and began to shoot at the zombies.

Violet excused herself from battle and quickly constructed a crude structure where her friends could spend the night. As she worked, she could see Hannah strike a vacant-eyed zombie with her diamond sword. Violet soon placed the final planks of wood and the house was completed. Then she carefully crafted beds for each of them. When she was finished with the beds, Noah walked through the door to the house.

"Wow, you did a really good job," he said.

"Thanks, Noah." Violet was pleased with her quick work. "I assume all of the zombies are destroyed?"

"Yes, they are gone," Noah replied.

Hannah and Ben walked into the small house. Ben remarked, "I placed a torch on the front of the house, so we won't have any more visitors."

"Good idea," Violet said. She realized she had forgotten to place a torch outside.

The group hopped into their beds and tried to sleep. Violet pulled the blue covers over her body and began to think about Will and Trent. She wondered where Daniel had taken them and if they were safe. The Overworld was massive—how would they ever find the treasure-hunting duo? Of course, she knew they had to focus on finding snow first, so the town could be safe. Violet drifted off to sleep dreaming about the ice plains and the many snowballs she would craft.

"It's morning," Hannah called out to the others, as the sun came through the small window.

"Great!" Noah exclaimed as he jumped out of bed. "We must eat and then make our way to the icy plains."

Hannah walked out of the house and began to hunt for meat. She spotted a chicken and shot an arrow. "We now have breakfast," Hannah announced proudly.

The group devoured the chicken and then began their trek toward the cold biome.

Noah studied the map and directed, "The icy plains are past the mountains to our left."

Ben paused and stared up at the massive mountains. "Do we have to climb those mountains?"

"I'm afraid so," Noah told his friend.

"But I'm afraid of heights." Ben was ashamed to admit this to the others.

"There's no better time to get over your fear of heights," Noah joked. "But seriously, we will be there with you. I know it's scary, but it will be a lot scarier if we return to our village without snowballs."

Hannah reassured Ben, "I know you're scared, but if we stick together, you'll make it up that mountain."

Ben's heart beat faster as they neared the mountains. With each step up the mountainside, he took a deep breath.

"Are you okay?" asked Violet.

Ben swallowed. His stomach felt like a million butterflies were swirling around in it. He was very scared. His palms were sweaty, but he replied, "I'll be fine. Let's keep going up the mountain."

"If you weren't afraid of heights, you'd love the view from the mountain." Violet looked out from the top of the mountain. She could see the town behind her and the icy plains stretched out in front of her.

Hannah looked at the icy plains and said to Ben, "We're almost there. I can see the icy plains. Once we get down the mountain, we'll be able to collect the snowballs."

"And then we have to travel all the way back up the mountain to get back to town?" Ben simply wanted this mountain adventure to end.

"Yes," Hannah replied. She knew there was nothing she could say to make Ben feel better. She just had to stay by his side while he traveled up and down the mountain and give him support.

The group hiked slowly down the mountain. The trail was very steep, and they were afraid they might fall. Once they reached the bottom, Ben let out a sigh of relief.

"See? It wasn't that bad, was it?" asked Violet.

"Truthfully?" Ben answered Violet honestly. "It was awful."

"I'm sure it was," said Noah, "but it was worth it. Look where we are."

The group had entered the icy plains. The white landscape seemed to go on forever. Hannah smiled and noted, "Wow, we can make a million snowballs. There's so much snow."

"I'm glad we made the trip," Ben said while he gathered a bunch of snow and began to craft snowballs. As the snowballs piled up in their inventories, the group was hopeful that they now could defeat the Nether mobs. And, in the meantime, they had crafted a plan.

Violet scanned the expansive icy biome and wondered where in the Overworld Will and Trent were being held prisoner. There were so many biomes and so many places to search. She was happy the group was building up a supply of snowballs to defeat the Nether mobs and Daniel, but without her treasure-hunting friends Will and Trent, she felt like this would be a cold and empty victory.

7

COLD FRONT

Watch out!" Noah warned Hannah, as she stepped onto a frozen river. "You could slip in!"

The group made its way very carefully through the icy and snowy biome. Violet could see tall ice formations in the distance. "Are those spikes?"

"Violet, I think you're right. Those are called ice spikes. They are very rare." Noah was excited to see ice spikes. They looked like upside-down icicles.

As the gang trekked through the frigid, frozen landscape, they picked up snow along the way.

Ben asked, "Do we really need to explore the spikes? Can't we just head back? My inventory is overflowing with snowballs, and I want to help the townspeople. We've been away too long."

Ben objected to investigating the ice plain's spikes because he wanted to get back over the mountain. Every minute they spent in the icy biome was another minute

Ben obsessed about the trip over the mountain. He imagined himself climbing up the side of the steep mountain—a thought which made his heart race. He wanted to be back home. He wanted to walk into town with the snowballs and hear the townspeople applaud their arrival. He wanted to be a hero. But right now, he was just plain scared of the trip back over the mountain.

The group didn't listen to Ben's protests, though. They were too excited as they headed for the ice spikes.

When they got close, they climbed the steps to touch them.

"These are so awesome!" Noah looked at the large spikes that rose from the blocks of snow.

"They're great. Can we leave now?" Ben was annoyed. He picked up another patch of snow and crafted a ball. "Am I the only one who is still making snowballs? You guys should be thinking about the townspeople."

Noah reached down and picked up some snow and made a snowball. "Yes, we care about the townspeople, but we also recognize that ice spikes are a very rare find in the Overworld. We want to investigate a little bit."

The spikes ranged in size. Some seemed so high that they were going to touch the sky. Violet gazed at the spikes in amazement. "These spikes are really cool, but Ben is right. We have to head back to the village."

Violet walked down the blocks and stepped carefully onto the frozen river. Hannah held Violet's hand as they made their way across the frozen waters.

Crack!

"What is that?" Violet asked nervously.

Hannah looked down and saw a large crack opening up in the frozen river. "Oh no! We are drifting away!"

"This never happens. Daniel must be setting a trap with command blocks," said Noah.

"But how does he know we're here?" asked Ben.

"It's an obvious place for us to be. He sent the Nether mobs and we needed snowballs. This is probably a booby trap," explained Noah.

The crack grew wider and the patch of ice Violet and Hannah stood on drifted out into the frozen river.

"Help us!" Violet called to Noah and Ben.

Noah and Ben looked for a tool to grab the ice with. They wanted to help their friends get back to shore.

Violet and Hannah drifted farther away. Noah called out, "We're trying to find something to help! Just wait!"

"We don't have time to wait!" Violet yelled back.

Hannah looked into her inventory. "I have an idea," she exclaimed.

"Great, what is it?" Violet was open to any ideas—she just wanted to get back to shore. They were floating farther away, and she worried they'd be stuck on the water for a very long time. As long as they were adrift, they couldn't help the townspeople and they certainly couldn't find Will and Trent.

Hannah handed Violet a potion of water breathing. "Drink this, and let's jump."

Violet took a large sip of the potion and jumped off the floating patch of ice. The water was cold as Violet swam to shore. Hannah led the way, and Violet swam closely behind. The two reached the shore and their friends cheered.

"I'm so happy that you're safe and that Daniel didn't destroy you." Noah smiled at his friends in relief.

"No thanks to you." Violet was annoyed that Noah hadn't saved them.

Noah defended himself. "I'm sorry, but it's hard to save someone who is floating away."

The gang stood on the shore of the cold beach. Hannah asked her friends, "Do we have enough snowballs for the townspeople now?"

The group gathered the last handfuls of remaining snow from the shoreline and began their journey back to the village.

Ben saw the dreaded mountain in the distance. The mountain loomed high above the ice plains. It overshadowed the large ice spikes in size. His heart began to beat faster with each step they took, drawing them nearer to the mountain.

"Are you nervous about going back up the mountain?" Hannah asked Ben.

He didn't want to admit he was still nervous, but he replied, "Yes, but I'll be fine. I have to think about the townspeople."

"Yes, and we have to think about finding Will and Trent," Violet added. Violet wondered where they were and if they were in a frigid biome like the ice plains. It was so barren and cold. She hoped the gang would be able to find them soon and set them free. They had to stop Daniel.

Noah glanced at his inventory before they made their climb up the enormous mountain. "I don't think I could fit another snowball in here if I tried."

The others checked their inventories and agreed. They all had inventories packed with snowballs and felt confident they had enough to defeat the Nether mobs that were attacking their village.

"I'm confident that we're going to win this battle against these mobs," Noah said as he took his first step up the side of the mountain.

Ben's heart pounded, and he wished he felt as confident as Noah. But Ben didn't realize that with each step, he was slowly overcoming his fear and gaining confidence.

When they reached the top of the mountain, the group was surprised when Ben looked out at the view and calmly announced, "I can see our village from up here."

Violet smiled at her friend, but her smile quickly disappeared when she heard a sinister laugh. The muted laugh sounded like it was coming from the direction of their town.

8
OUR TOWN

After climbing the mountain twice, Ben felt confident and proud as he strode into the village with an inventory overflowing with snowballs. Before he could enjoy the satisfaction of overcoming his lifelong fear of heights, though, he spotted Daniel standing in the center of town, ordering the rainbow griefers to attack the townspeople.

Violet rushed toward Daniel and struck him with her enchanted diamond sword.

Daniel just laughed. He grabbed a potion from his inventory and gulped it down. "You think you're going to destroy me?"

Violet struck Daniel again, but he hit Violet with his diamond sword. Violet didn't realize she had spent all of her energy in the cold ice plains, and she was destroyed. She respawned in the house she had built, which was located outside of the town.

Violet felt panicked when she respawned in her bed. She was alone, and it was a half-day journey back to the town. She crawled out of bed and began to eat some potatoes to regain her energy.

"Violet," Noah called from the bed. He had just respawned, too.

"What's happening in the town? I'm upset that we are so far away," Violet spoke rapidly and began to pace around the small house.

"I think the others will respawn here soon," Noah said. He sounded defeated as he spoke. "We let our energy bars reach dangerously low levels, and now we are paying the price. We sacrificed a lot to get those snowballs."

"But we needed them," Violet reminded her friend.

"Yes, we did. Also, Daniel is fighting a very tough battle. He has amassed another army. This one is much larger than the last. He even has silver griefers that are extremely skilled fighters. I was destroyed by a silver griefer."

Violet paced restlessly. "Silver griefers? Wow, I'll have to really watch out for them."

Hannah and Ben respawned at almost the same exact moment. Violet looked at them as they awoke in their beds.

"Wow, we're all here," Ben mumbled. He sounded groggy.

"We have to go back to the village, and we have to do it quickly," Hannah stated as she arose from the bed.

Violet handed Hannah a potato. "We need to slow down and regain our strength or we will just be destroyed again and will respawn in this house."

The group devoured the potatoes, and Noah said, "We must come up with a plan. We shouldn't just stroll into town—that will leave us open for another attack."

Violet agreed. "We have to think of a way to trick Daniel and his evil rainbow griefer army."

"And now he has those serious silver griefers, too," added Ben.

Ben and Noah began to discuss the skilled silver griefers. As they talked, Noah suggested, "Maybe we should change our skin to silver. Daniel will think we are the silver griefers."

"We've done that before," remarked Violet. It was true. They had dressed up as rainbow griefers to confuse Daniel in a previous battle. It had worked in the past, but Violet realized that Daniel was smart. They needed a new plan.

Hannah agreed with Violet. "Also, there were only a couple of silver griefers in his army. Daniel would realize that more silver griefers had appeared. He would definitely be suspicious."

Violet paused and asked, "Did you say . . . only two silver griefers?"

"Yes. There are only two," confirmed Ben.

"Do you think Daniel has changed Will and Trent into the two silver griefers?" Violet asked her friends.

"But if he did, why would Will and Trent hurt us? They are our friends." Ben didn't understand.

"I was destroyed by a silver griefer," added Hannah.

Violet couldn't stop fixating on the fact that there were only two silver griefers in all of Daniel's army. "Maybe Daniel brainwashed them."

Noah said, "Maybe you're right. But what can we do to save them or change them back to our old treasure-hunting friends?"

"I'm not sure. But I think I have a plan." Then Violet asked, "Hannah, do you have any potion of invisibility in your inventory?"

Hannah checked and replied, "Yes, I do. And I have more than enough for all of us."

"Great!" said Violet. "We will enter the town, but we will be invisible."

"But when we're invisible, we can't wear armor. After the potion wears off, we'll be open targets. We'll be destroyed in seconds," said Hannah.

"We will have to take that chance," Violet spoke slowly. She was still figuring out the details of the plan. "Maybe we can hide once we become visible. If we do that we will have time to put on our armor."

"Once we drink the potion and become invisible, what do we do?" asked Ben.

"I want us to target the two silver griefers," replied Violet. "I want to find out if they are actually Will and Trent. If they are, I think we have a serious chance of defeating Daniel."

"How?" asked Ben.

"Obviously Daniel has control over them. Once we let them know they are safe with us, they'll join *us* in battle." Violet seemed to think this was a great plan.

"What happens if they are truly brainwashed, though, and want to stick with Daniel?" Noah was worried that their old friends might destroy them instead of joining them.

"I guess that's a chance we'll have to take," Violet said as she walked out of the house and started the journey back to the village.

"You really think those silver griefers are Will and Trent?" asked Hannah.

"Yes, and I'm sure they'll help us defeat Daniel," replied Violet.

Violet was hopeful her plan would work and that they would save the town and their treasure-hunting friends. But before the gang could put their plan into action, they were attacked by three white ghasts that flew past them.

"Watch out!" Noah screamed as he dodged the flying fireball that almost struck him.

The gang took out their snowballs and aimed at the ghasts. Violet could swear she heard a shrill laugh booming from behind her, but she couldn't look back, because she had to battle the menacing ghasts.

9
DODGING BLASTS

Ghasts and blazes!" Hannah shrieked as she eyed the mobs and threw snowballs.

"And magma cubes!" cried Violet.

The gang dug into their large supply of snowballs to battle the flying Nether mobs. Hannah and Violet fought the magma cubes that pounced at them.

"We're never going to make it back to the town. This is intense!" Ben called out as he slammed a ghast with a snowball.

Noah was aiming at a yellow blaze when he was struck by a fiery blast and was destroyed.

"At least he's going to respawn in the house that is right behind us," Ben noted as he hit another ghast and destroyed it.

The magma cubes, with their dark red skin and menacing orange eyes, leaped at Hannah and Violet. Violet struck one with her sword, and it broke into smaller cubes. Hannah destroyed the smaller cubes.

"We make a great team," Hannah commented as she picked up the magma cream the magma cubes had dropped. She placed the cream in her inventory and said, "This will come in handy when brewing potions of fire resistance."

"And we'll need that!" Ben shouted as he dodged a blast from a blaze.

With the magma cubes destroyed, the gang turned their attention to the ghasts and blazes that flew through the sky.

"It's getting dark," Hannah warned as they threw snowballs at the flying Nether mobs.

"I think we have it!" exclaimed Ben as one of the last ghasts was destroyed.

When the sky was free of hostile mobs, the group hurried back to the town. Once the village streets were in sight, they paused and Hannah handed out the potion of invisibility.

Hannah counted slowly, "One . . . two . . . three." On three, the group swallowed the potion.

"I can't see you," Ben said in a panic.

"That's the point," Hannah laughed.

"But how can we keep track of each other?" Ben wasn't sure this plan was going to work.

"Let's run toward the center of town," instructed Violet. "When we spot the silver griefers, don't let them out of our sight."

The group sprinted into town. The town was in the thick of battle. Violet could hear snippets of conversations from the townspeople. One townsperson was battling a red rainbow griefer while asking, "Where are Noah and Violet? They said they'd protect us."

Another townsperson cried, "They left so long ago! They said they'd return with snowballs. If they don't return, we're going to lose this battle."

Violet didn't like hearing the townspeople question their plan. Violet and her friends were only trying to help. But she understood that the villagers were frustrated. They had been fighting a nonstop battle, and they were exhausted.

Noah also heard the townspeople talking about them. He wanted to discuss all of this with Violet. Of course, he knew that once he opened his mouth, there would be no point in being invisible. So he kept quiet and just looked for the silver griefers.

Violet finally spotted the two silver griefers. They stood atop Valentino's butcher shop and shot arrows at the townspeople. Their aim was excellent, and they were able to destroy hordes of townspeople while they attempted to defend themselves.

The gang climbed on top of Valentino's butcher shop. Violet spoke softly, "Will . . ."

The silver griefer turned around and spoke to his friend, "Did you say something?"

"No," replied the other silver griefer.

"Will . . ." Violet spoke again.

"Okay, someone *is* talking." The silver griefer was annoyed.

"What did the voice say?" asked the other griefer.

"They called out the name Will."

The silver griefer asked, "Isn't that the name of the guy Daniel has trapped in his desert palace?"

"Yes!" he replied as he aimed and shot arrows at the townspeople.

"That's weird," the other griefer said as he also shot a barrage of arrows at the sea of innocent people.

It was then that Violet realized these two silver griefers were *not* her friends. This made her feel so much better. Even if her friends were brainwashed, she would be very upset if they had turned so evil and had destroyed innocent townspeople.

Now that the plan had changed, Violet had to destroy these two evil silver griefers.

"Destroy them!" she called out to her friends.

The silver griefers didn't have time to figure out where the voice was coming from because within seconds, they were attacked by invisible people carrying enchanted diamond swords.

As the two silver griefers disappeared, the gang began to reappear. There are very few times in life when one has perfect timing. This was one of those times. The townspeople were in awe and began to cheer for Violet, Noah, Hannah, and Ben. Unfortunately, the gang didn't have time to enjoy the applause because they had an agenda. They put on their armor, jumped down from the roof of the butcher shop, and attacked the remaining rainbow griefers.

As Noah struck one of the last rainbow griefers, he asked the orange griefer, "Where is Daniel?"

"You'll never find out," the griefer called back with a laugh, and Noah struck him again. He was destroyed.

Noah didn't have any answers. They still had to find Daniel and had no clue where he was.

Violet stepped up next to Noah in battle, and as she struck a green griefer she said, "I think Daniel is in the desert."

"Really?" Noah asked as he destroyed another griefer.

"Yes, I heard the silver griefers talking about Will and Trent being trapped in a desert palace."

"But there are tons of desert biomes in the Overworld. How will we find the one that houses Daniel's palace?"

Violet said, "We should check the desert outside of our town. I bet that's where he's hiding with Will and Trent."

"I hope you're right," replied Noah.

As Violet struck a pink griefer with her enchanted diamond sword, she heard the griefer utter the words, "You are right," before it was destroyed.

"That griefer is trying to help us," Violet told Noah.

"I don't trust griefers, but I do think we should look there first," said Noah.

The final griefer was soon destroyed. The townspeople applauded.

Noah stood in the center of the town and announced, "We have to travel to the desert. But we want to distribute snowballs to everyone in the town first, in case the ghasts and magma cubes come back."

The townspeople lined up and received their snowballs. They had protection now against the Nether mobs. Noah made sure the gang still had some snowballs, too. They had no way of knowing what Nether mobs they might encounter on the road to the desert.

10
TREASURE OR TRAP?

The desert wasn't far from the village. As the gang set out on their trip, Valentino the Butcher hurried toward them. "Hey!" he called out. "You need to take this meat and eat it for energy."

"Do you want us to trade anything for the meat?" Noah asked. He had a few emeralds and some wheat in his inventory and would gladly trade them for the meat.

"No," replied Valentino. "I just want to help you all. You have done so much for our village, and you deserve this food."

The gang thanked Valentino. They stopped and ate the tasty meat, and watched as their health bars increased. Then they set out toward the desert.

On the way, the friends had to pass through a lush jungle. Noah reminded his friends, "The jungle has many areas where it's so overgrown with leaves that we might lose our way and not find each other."

"Yes," said Hannah, "we must stick together."

Ben added, "If we didn't lose each other when we were invisible, I'm sure we'll be able to stick together in the jungle."

Noah was glad everyone had the same thought. "Good. And once we get to the desert, we need to track down Daniel and destroy him."

"Yes," said Violet, "and we also have to free Will and Trent. I wonder what Daniel is doing to them. Those poor guys are trapped in his desert palace. Daniel is probably starving them."

"We'll save them!" declared Noah.

Hannah sheared the leafy tree-lined path, as they trekked deeper into the dense jungle.

"Do you see that?" Violet asked her friends.

Around a bend in the path, the gang saw a jungle temple that was extremely lavish. The large structure was located on a stretch of water. A large arch framed the entrance to the waterfront temple. Although they had to concentrate and make it to the desert before dark, they were also struck by the temple's total awesomeness.

"Should we go in?" asked Hannah.

Noah paused and stated, "It looks so grand, and maybe we'll find treasure there, but it's almost night. We have to stick to our plan of reaching the desert."

Violet agreed with Noah, but she didn't want to pass up this opportunity of entering a jungle temple. "Maybe we can just stop in for a quick look?"

The rest of the gang also wanted to search the temple. Ben said, "If we do go and find treasure, we can put that in our inventory and it might come in handy when we're battling Daniel and his evil rainbow griefer army."

Everyone admitted that they really did want to enter the temple. The friends went off course and walked toward the temple. They looked up as they passed beneath the arch that stood in front of the grand temple.

Violet was the first to enter the temple. "Maybe I'll finally get to go on the treasure hunt I always wanted to!"

Noah asked, "Does anybody know where treasures are hidden in jungle temples?"

Without their treasure-hunting friends Will and Trent leading them, the group had to navigate their own way around. They explored the temple and peeked into the many rooms to search for treasure chests.

"I don't think the treasure chests are just left out in the rooms. I think we have to go to the bottom floor and unearth the chests," Violet said. She remembered Will and Trent telling her a story about treasure hunting in the jungle. They had mentioned how they unearthed booby-trapped treasure.

"Yes, I remember Will and Trent telling us a story about finding treasure," Noah told them.

"Right," Violet exclaimed. "I was just thinking about that story. Hopefully we'll remember enough of the details they told us to help on this impromptu treasure hunt."

The dimly lit temple was a breeding ground for hostile mobs to spawn, especially in the temple's darker secret rooms. The gang walked into a secret room, hoping it was where they'd find the treasure, but instead they found lots of silverfish.

"Yuck!" Violet called out as she was attacked by dozens of small insects that slithered on the ground of the secret room.

The gang used their swords to fight the small hostile mobs. As they struggled with the insect mob, a skeleton rattled down the hall toward them.

Click! Clack! Clang!

The skeleton wasn't alone. Violet looked up and saw five skeletons coming toward them. One of the skeleton's arrows struck Violet's armor, and she dashed toward the bony beasts with her enchanted diamond sword.

The others continued to battle the silverfish invasion. Violet was fighting the skeletons on her own. A skeleton's arrow pierced her arm. She grew weaker and needed help. Hannah ran into the thick of the battle and used her sword to destroy a skeleton. As the duo obliterated two skeletons, they noticed more skeletons coming down the stairs.

"We need more help!" Violet called to Noah and Ben.

"We're almost done with the silverfish. Ben found the spawner!" Noah called out.

Violet and Hannah were shocked when three people rushed down the stairs and annihilated all of the skeletons.

"Who are you?" asked Violet.

"We're treasure hunters," replied a boy wearing a gold helmet.

"Who are *you?*" questioned the treasure hunter who was wearing a pink helmet.

"I'm Violet."

"And I'm Hannah. And we're not treasure hunters."

"Violet and Hannah. Are you friends with Will and Trent?" asked the treasure hunter wearing a blue helmet.

"Yes." Violet was shocked. Noah and Ben walked over and introduced themselves, too.

The boy wearing the gold helmet said, "I'm Henry."

The boy wearing the blue helmet added, "I'm Max."

And the girl in the pink helmet said, "I'm Lucy."

Violet exclaimed, "We've heard so many stories about you! It's great to finally meet you!"

"We feel the same way about you," replied Lucy.

"But we have awful news," Violet told the treasure hunters. "Will and Trent are trapped in a desert palace."

"What? That's horrible!" Henry was upset.

"An evil griefer named Daniel has trapped them," said Violet.

"We know Daniel. He is really wicked," said Lucy.

"Can you help us free them?" asked Noah.

Suddenly, the treasure they had been seeking seemed to lose its importance. The gang needed to save Will and Trent. So they all left the temple without treasure, but with something more valuable than diamonds—they left with new friends.

11
REUNITED

I can't believe we left the temple without finding any treasure," Violet lamented as the gang headed toward the desert.

"Once we free Will and Trent, we promise to take you on a treasure-hunting adventure," Henry said as he sheared a path through the jungle.

"Thanks." Violet was excited to have met these famed treasure hunters. Will and Trent always told exciting tales about Henry, Max, and Lucy.

"What are we going to do once we reach the desert? Do we have a plan?" asked Henry.

"I think we're just going to charge into the desert palace and save Will and Trent." As she spoke, Violet realized this plan seemed pretty ridiculous.

"I think you're going to need a better strategy," said Max, and then he added, "I hope that didn't come across as sounding rude. I just want to make sure we save our friends."

"No, I think you're right. We are going to need a better plan," Violet agreed.

Night was now setting in. Lucy told the gang, "We don't travel at night. It's too dangerous."

Noah said, "We all need a place to stay for the night. Fortunately, Violet is one of the best builders in the Overworld."

"Will told us about Violet's stellar building skills," said Lucy. "I can't wait to see her in action. We also have a friend, Steve, who is a master builder. We once went to a building competition that he was invited to on Mooshroom Island."

"Wow, that's an impressive competition," remarked Violet as she grabbed planks to form her inventory so she could build a house for the night. "I've always wanted to participate in that one, but I've never gotten a chance to make it."

The gang helped Violet build the house outside the desert. Lucy said, "You didn't miss much. The competition was intense."

Max added, "There was an Endermen invasion. We spent the entire time fighting Endermen and endermites."

Ben was confused. "I thought hostile mobs don't spawn on Mooshroom Island."

Henry remembered the craziness of the building competition on Mooshroom Island and said, "They don't usually. This was an odd case."

The group worked together to build a shelter for the night. Violet placed the roof on at last, and the gang entered the house before sunset.

"You did such a great job. Will and Trent are right. You are truly talented, Violet. They told us about your tree house and how it has amazing views and is so large that it's nestled in two trees," complimented Henry.

"When we find our friends and save them, I want you to come visit our town and stay in my tree house," Violet said as she crafted beds for everyone.

"It's a deal. We take you on an official treasure hunt, and you let us stay in your tree house!" exclaimed Lucy.

The weary friends climbed into their beds. They quickly fell asleep with blue wool blankets draped over their tired bodies.

Morning came quickly. The sun was shining and the group was excited to start their trip to the desert.

Noah offered their new friends the extra meat he had from Valentino the Butcher.

As Max ate breakfast he told them about Lucy's incredible hunting skills.

Lucy said, "You exaggerate," but she felt pleased.

The group finished their food and exited the house. The desert could be seen in the distance. As they reached the sandy biome, a ghast flew toward them and shot a fireball.

"Ghasts?" Max was confused.

"In the Overworld?" questioned Henry.

"Daniel is behind this Nether mob invasion," Noah warned them as he struck the ghast with a snowball.

"Bull's-eye!" Max called out. "You did a good job destroying that ghast."

"Should we be worried that there are more Nether mobs ready to attack us? And in daylight?" Henry was clearly upset.

"Once we defeat Daniel, we'll be able to stop him from summoning the Nether mobs," said Violet.

"You talk like that's an easy thing to do," Max protested as he walked toward the desert.

The desert palace stood out in the flat terrain. The enormous palace was four stories high with a large terrace across the front of the building. A cactus garden with a table and chairs could be seen on the side of the palace.

"How are you going to get inside?" asked Max.

Violet looked over at Hannah for a solution. Hannah took out the last of her potion of invisibility. "Take off your armor," she instructed.

The gang reluctantly took off their armor and drank the potion. The group ran toward the desert palace and entered the lavish structure without any of the rainbow griefers noticing them. They were all completely invisible. They raced throughout the house, searching for the room where Daniel had trapped their friends.

They rushed down the stairs to the basement. They sprinted down a long hallway until they saw a closed door. Two rainbow griefers stood guard in front of the door. Noah took out his sword and pierced the rainbow guard. The other guard looked shocked. Noah struck the second guard. He destroyed them both. Ben opened the door, and the gang ran inside.

Although they were invisible, their voices could still be heard. When they saw Will and Trent they called out their names: "Will! Trent!"

"Violet!" cried Trent.

"Max?" Will sounded confused.

"Are all of our friends here?" Trent asked. He was overjoyed.

Noah spoke up. "There's no time for happy reunions. Hannah, please give them some potion of invisibility so we can get out of here."

Hannah stammered, "I—I don't have any left."

12

DISTRACTIONS IN THE DESERT

How will we escape if we aren't all invisible?" Noah asked.

"I have an idea," announced Violet. She took out blocks of TNT from her inventory and placed them on the floor. "Can somebody ignite this? It will be a great distraction."

Max ignited the TNT, and the group dashed out of the room before the harsh blast.

Kaboom!

The gang hurried up the stairs as the rainbow griefers raced toward the blast. They didn't even notice Will and Trent on the stairs because they were so concerned about the explosion.

"What could that be?" Violet heard one of the rainbow griefers question.

They ran out of the palace and sprinted through the desert. As they went along, the potion slowly wore off. As it did, rainbow griefers sprinted out of the palace toward them.

"They got away!" a blue griefer called out, and he shot arrows at them.

"And they have their friends with them!" a green griefer screamed as he ran after them with his diamond sword.

"Tell Daniel," the silver griefer called out. "He has to annihilate these prisoners and their friends."

"Yes," the blue griefer laughed. "Hardcore mode for all of these creepers."

The gang raced as fast as they could, but they were losing energy. They didn't have any potion of invisibility left and the journey back to the town would take a while. There was no way they would make it if they had these rainbow griefers trailing them.

Noah suggested, "Maybe we should teleport?"

"Good idea," replied Violet.

"But we don't know where we have to teleport to? We've never been to your village," explained Lucy.

"That isn't a good option then," said Will.

Trent saw a bus out of the corner of his eye. "The bus!" he exclaimed.

The group boarded the bus, and Trent used command blocks to drive as fast as he could to the village. Violet looked out the window. The rainbow griefers weren't in sight. "I think we're going to make it," she said happily.

The bus drove through the sandy flat desert dotted with cacti and into the lush green forest. It passed the jungle temple. Will and Trent pointed out the large structure.

"We can't stop now," Violet told them. "We have to get back to the village. And it's too risky with Daniel following us."

Lucy added, "That's the temple where we met you guys."

Henry said, "As I said, once we defeat Daniel, I will take you on a treasure-hunting expedition."

"That sounds like fun," remarked Violet as she held onto her seat on the bumpy bus ride.

The bus reached the outskirts of their village just as six blazes flew directly at the them.

"Get out!" exclaimed Trent. "The bus is going to explode!"

The group exited before the fireballs struck the bus and it burst into flames.

"We made it out just in time." Violet watched as flames engulfed the vehicle.

Suddenly, Valentino joined them. "You're back!" He was very excited to see his old friends. "It's been a harsh battle against the Nether mobs. Every time we defeat them with snowballs, more spawn."

"I think we're about to be attacked by rainbow griefers, too," Noah warned Valentino.

"They're mad because we freed Will and Trent," added Violet.

Valentino stared at Henry, Max, and Lucy. "Who are you?" He was suspicious of any newcomers. He had the right to be wary of new people, especially since Otto had turned out to be a traitor.

"I'm Lucy. These are my friends, Henry and Max."

Will said, "They have been good friends of mine for a long time. They helped save me."

"Me, too," added Trent. "We were trapped in the basement of a desert palace in a dark room, where we were constantly attacked by silverfish."

"That sounds awful," said Valentino.

Violet interrupted, "Seriously, this is no time for introductions and backstories. There are ghasts and blazes flying over the town."

"And large cubes!" Valentino added.

"I'll deal with the magma cubes," Hannah offered. She felt like a magma cube expert since she had defeated countless cubes with just one strike from her diamond sword.

The group hurried into town. When they arrived, they were surprised to see the silver griefers still attacking the townspeople. The two silver griefers were striking innocent people with their diamond swords.

"Stop!" Noah called to the silver griefers.

The griefers laughed, and one of them screamed, "It would be our pleasure to destroy you!"

"Never!" Noah rushed toward the griefers and struck one of them with his diamond sword.

Violet shot an arrow at the other griefer, but it was too late. The griefers had destroyed Noah. He respawned in the little house outside of the desert. Violet imagined him all alone. She wanted to go to the house and save him.

"Violet, watch out!" shouted Hannah.

Violet tried to avoid the arrow that was flying in her direction. She stepped back, but a fireball destroyed her.

Violet respawned in the house. "Noah?" she shouted as she looked for her friend.

"Violet?" Noah called out. He was standing outside the house. His arrow was aimed at a chicken.

"We need to get back to our village!"

Noah successfully hunted down the chicken and offered some to Violet. She thanked him for the food.

"I have a plan," he reassured Violet as they finished eating.

"Okay, but we must get back. We don't have much time." Violet was worried about the townspeople and her friends who were battling the Nether mobs and the silver griefers by themselves.

"Let's teleport," Noah told his friend.

And in an instant they were back home.

13
RAINBOW LAVA

They're throwing lava!" Hannah pointed out to Noah as he and Violet arrived in the center of town.

Suddenly Daniel appeared. He stood in the center of town laughing as his rainbow griefer army marched down the street carrying buckets of lava. They threw the lava on townspeople and used some lava to flood shops and homes.

"We have to stop them!" Noah called out.

"How?" Violet was scared. She didn't want to be destroyed by lava.

"We don't want to destroy the town," added Hannah. "We have to be very careful."

Just then, a ghast flew at Violet. Before the fireball could strike her, she threw a snowball at the flying menace and destroyed it.

Noah rushed to help his friends. He shouted at Daniel and his army, "This is it! This war is over! Leave our town alone!"

Daniel laughed defiantly. "After what you've done to me? Never!"

Otto appeared and charged at Noah. He hit Noah with his diamond sword and destroyed him.

"I'll keep destroying Noah and the rest of you until I've annihilated this town off the map." Daniel laughed again—and this time the laugh was even deeper and more sinister.

"Not on my watch," warned Violet. She grabbed a bucket of lava from one of the griefers and threw it on Daniel. He was instantly destroyed.

"You've destroyed him, you evil person!" Otto screamed at Violet.

"He deserved it." Violet was happy with her victory, but she assumed it was short-lived. Daniel was probably going to teleport into the center of town to retaliate at any minute.

Otto held his diamond sword against Violet's neck. "You have caused enough trouble," he threatened.

"I thought you were my friend, Otto. When we met in the Nether, you were so friendly. I have no idea why you changed."

"I was just pretending to be nice. I was waiting for Daniel to give me instructions on how to destroy you."

"Why do you need instructions from Daniel? He's just a bully. Can't you think for yourself?"

Otto stood, silent. Then he slammed his sword against Violet's arm. It pierced her, and she lost some hearts.

"Stop it, Otto!" Violet said. "You aren't a griefer. You don't even have rainbow skin. You're still wearing your black suit. Why don't you just be your own person?"

"Violet, you are really bothering me," Otto said, and he struck her again. Violet's health bar was growing weaker as she lost more hearts.

Violet wanted Otto to think for himself, but she also wanted to survive. She grabbed another bucket of lava from a pink griefer and splashed it on Otto. He was destroyed instantly.

"You've destroyed Daniel and Otto," one of the townspeople called out. "You are our hero!"

"The battle isn't over." Violet pointed to the ghasts flying through the sky and the many griefers carrying lava buckets. "We still need to fight."

Violet threw snowballs, but she knew this wasn't a real plan. She and her friends were just treading water. They needed an effective plan, one that would end this Nether mob invasion once and for all.

Noah and Ben kept busy battling the lava-carrying griefers. They struck them with arrows. They were doing a good job, and there were only a handful of griefers left. Just as they were about to destroy one of the last griefers, Noah and Ben were destroyed in a surprise attack.

They hadn't noticed the two silver griefers creeping up behind them. The silver griefers struck them with their diamond swords. As Noah and Ben turned around to defend themselves, the silver griefers threw lava on them.

Noah respawned in the small house Violet had built. Ben respawned next to him.

"What are we going to do? I don't want to go back there unless we have a plan," Ben complained.

Noah looked out the window. The sky grew dark. "It's almost nighttime. I think this is going to be an ultimate battle. Soon the regular hostile mobs of the Overworld will spawn, and we will have to fight them, too."

"What is your plan?" Ben was hopeful Noah could save the day.

"I think we need to trap the griefers," Noah told him. "Now, let's teleport."

The town was in shambles, but the rainbow griefers were all destroyed. Violet rushed over to her friends with the good news. "We've destroyed all the griefers."

Hannah added, "For now, that is. I'm sure they'll be back."

The townspeople destroyed the remaining Nether mobs that lurked in the town. There was a rare silence as the night began to set in.

Noah made an announcement: "We must build a jail."

Violet was perplexed. "Why?"

"We need to trap the griefers. If we destroy them, they will just respawn. Once we have them trapped, we can find Daniel and trap him, too. That will prevent him from summoning any more Nether mobs."

Violet wasn't sure Noah's idea would work, but there wasn't any other plan.

"Should we go home since it's dusk and we don't want to be attacked by hostile mobs?" one of the townspeople questioned.

"I'm sorry, but we can't. We must help Violet construct a large jail. One that would be impossible to escape from," said Noah.

Violet didn't want to admit that she was excited about this building project. It was an unusual project for her. The only time she had built a prison was when she once created a small bedrock house to trap Daniel in. Violet took supplies from her inventory and began to build the foundation for the jail.

The townspeople crowded around Violet, and she gave orders on what needed to be constructed. Noah and Ben kept a lookout for hostile mobs of the Overworld that spawned in the darkness.

Violet and the townspeople were making progress on the jail when Noah screamed out, "Zombie attack!"

14
GHASTLY CREEPERS

The zombies weren't the real trouble, though. Noah didn't see the silent creepers that came up behind him and ignited themselves. Noah and Ben were instantly destroyed.

The townspeople halted construction on the jail and battled the gang of zombies lumbering toward them.

"Look up!" Lucy screamed, as a ghast shot a fireball down at them.

"We have snowballs," exclaimed Henry, and he pitched them at the flying Nether mob.

A cluster of creepers swarmed into the town and exploded near some townspeople.

"I don't know who to fight first," Violet called out, as she held a diamond sword in one hand and a snowball in the other.

"At least we don't have to battle any rainbow griefers right now," said Hannah.

"You always look on the bright side," said Violet, praising her friend.

Snowballs flew through the night sky. Townspeople dodged blasts while they tried not to be destroyed by the tricky silent creepers that were spawning all over the town.

Noah and Ben teleported back to the town after they respawned and continued their battle against the zombies.

"Ouch!" cried Lucy. She was expecting to see a skeleton, but she was surprised to see an orange rainbow griefer standing in front of her. He aimed his bow and arrow at Lucy, and she was hit by another arrow.

"Griefers!" Lucy warned the others.

Ben lit a torch and placed it outside Valentino's butcher shop. He spotted Valentino inside the shop. "Save us!" Valentino called out to his friend.

"I'm trying!" Ben replied.

Fireballs fell onto the townspeople. Zombies ripped the doors off houses. Creepers exploded. Rainbow griefers shot arrows at everyone. It was total and utter chaos. Noah tried to come up with an alternate plan as he fought a griefer. Soon after the skeletons marched into town and began to shoot arrows, the sun came up. The hostile mobs from the Overworld disappeared. The group only had to battle the Nether mobs and the griefers.

Violet looked at the jail. She just needed to complete the roof and the building would be finished, but she wasn't sure how she'd be able to do it. There were too many distractions, too many battles.

The group was shocked when Daniel strolled into the town. He walked over to Violet and said, "Ah. You were planning on trapping me again, weren't you?" Daniel inspected the jail and said with a smirk, "Don't you remember that I escaped from your bedrock prison? You can't trap me!"

Violet used all of her might to strike Daniel with her diamond sword. He lost a few hearts, but he still had energy left. He reached for his sword, and Violet screamed, "Help me!"

The entire town rushed at Daniel and destroyed him.

"Now you can finish the jail," Noah said to Violet.

Violet carried supplies to the jail, and a bunch of townspeople helped her. They were determined to build a prison to securely house the evil griefers. Violet placed the roof on the building as Noah began to force the griefers into a temporary jail in a small house in the village.

At first it was hard to get the griefers to enter the temporary jail, but when Noah threatened them with hot lava, they quickly dashed into the house.

"We have six rainbow griefers in the house," Henry told Violet.

Violet finally completed the new jail. "Bring the rainbow griefers over here. I have jail cells for all of them."

Lucy, Max, and Henry held buckets of lava ready as Noah marched the imprisoned griefers toward their new home—a jailhouse.

Every time a griefer looked like he was ready to run, Lucy reminded him that she was carrying hot lava and she wasn't afraid to use it.

"You did this to yourselves," Noah told the griefers. "If you didn't follow Daniel, you wouldn't be a prisoner."

Otto suddenly appeared in the town and shouted to the griefers, "Fight back! Don't go to jail!"

The griefers looked at Otto. The griefers looked at the lava. They kept marching after Noah.

"Don't let them win!" Otto screamed as he raced toward Noah with his diamond sword.

A ghast flew at both of them. Noah jumped back and narrowly avoided being destroyed by the fireball. Otto, however, was destroyed.

Noah continued to lead the group of griefers to their new home. Once they reached the jailhouse, Violet said, "Each one of you gets a window. When this battle with Daniel is over, I want you to see how a normal, peaceful village operates. I want you to look out this window and see people working together to build a community. Yes, we occasionally argue with each other, but we don't summon Nether mobs to destroy innocent people. We don't join an army obedient to a man who once tried to destroy our Olympic games and our amusement park. We think for ourselves, and we are free. You'll get to see that every day and realize what you are missing. That will be the biggest punishment of all."

The griefers were marched into their cells. Suddenly, Daniel appeared and called out, "What a great speech, Violet."

"Daniel?" Violet was shocked. She instructed the townspeople to lock the jail cells quickly so the griefers couldn't escape and help Daniel.

"Yes, it's me." Daniel laughed.

"And me, Otto." He had appeared in his black suit, wearing armor and holding a diamond sword.

"You have led these people to a life of imprisonment," Violet stated, pointing at the griefers in the jail. She held her sword tightly and pointed it at Daniel.

Noah and the others stood behind Violet. All were armored up and holding their swords.

"You're not going to win this time, Daniel," said Will.

"Oh Will, why did all of your treasure-hunter friends join forces with Violet and Noah? Why couldn't they be smart like Otto and stick with a winner?" Daniel laughed again.

"Smart?" Lucy called out. "I think joining your army was the worst thing Otto could have done."

Otto looked at Lucy and winced. Her words seemed to impact him.

"Otto, destroy her!" ordered Daniel.

Lucy was terrified. She didn't want to be destroyed and respawn alone in the house near the desert. Her heart skipped a beat. She waited for Otto to destroy her, but he didn't move.

15
TIME-OUT

Otto shocked everyone when he rushed toward Daniel and hit him with his diamond sword.

"Otto? What are you doing?" Daniel gasped as he tried to fight back.

"Don't destroy Daniel," Noah called out to Otto.

Otto was confused. "But I want to destroy him. He's evil!"

"Destroying him won't solve anything. It's better to put him in this jailhouse," explained Violet.

"I'll never go into that jail!" Daniel screamed. "I'd rather be destroyed."

The townspeople gathered around Daniel and trapped him. They marched him to the jailhouse while he protested all the way. But nobody listened. Violet led Daniel toward his jail cell.

"Did you hear my speech about the window?" asked Violet.

"Spare me the speeches," Daniel replied angrily as Violet closed the gate to the jail cell and looked at him through the bars.

"Daniel, now you will have time to think about all the bad things you've done to us." Violet continued. "And you'll get to watch us rebuild and live the life we want to live."

Daniel shouted, "Not for long! I am going to escape and destroy this village. You can't keep me trapped in here."

Nobody listened to Daniel's protests. As Violet stepped outside the jailhouse, a blaze shot a fireball at her. She was destroyed.

"Violet!" Noah cried out. He was devastated. Noah raced back into the jailhouse and stood in front of Daniel's cell.

Daniel laughed. "Your friend was destroyed."

"You need to stop the Nether mobs," Noah demanded.

"Not unless you free me."

"I'll never free you, but this is a warning—you must stop summoning the Nether mobs."

"I love this little window that Violet built for each cell. Now each day I get to watch as your town is destroyed by Nether mobs. Maybe I was wrong. Being in prison might be fun, especially given the fantastic view."

Noah was infuriated. "If you don't stop summoning the Nether mobs, I will force you to stop."

Daniel replied with a laugh. "And how will you do that?"

Noah grabbed a bucket of lava and held it up against the bars. "I am going to flood your cell with lava. It's going to be very hot and will destroy you."

"And then you'll have to find me when I respawn in the Overworld. Within a short while, I'll have a new and stronger army, and we'll stage another attack on your town."

Noah was shaken by the thought of Daniel getting the better of him. And he had no clue how to convince Daniel to stop summoning the mobs. Maybe the town would just learn to live with these constant attacks? Noah wasn't sure what to do next.

As if in answer to his dilemma, Lucy walked into the jailhouse.

"Look out the window." She smiled as she spoke to Daniel.

Daniel stared out the window. "I don't see anything."

"Exactly," Lucy chuckled. "There aren't any Nether mobs terrorizing the town with their fiery explosions."

"What?" Daniel was shocked.

Lucy explained to Noah, "Daniel wasn't the one summoning the Nether mobs. He had someone in the desert palace calling for the Nether mobs with command blocks. Otto told us all about it. Otto teleported back to the desert and stopped the attack."

Daniel was speechless.

"It's over now, Daniel," Lucy stated calmly.

"You can't terrorize us anymore," said Violet. She was happy to be back with the gang after respawning.

Daniel looked out the window at the quiet town. He tried to think of a way to escape from the jailhouse, but he couldn't come up with a good plan. He simply stared out the window and watched as the town worked together to rebuild. He shuddered at the thought of people working together. Daniel liked to destroy things.

"Maybe sitting in here and having a time-out will be good for you," Violet said to the silent Daniel.

"Yes, it will give me time to stage my next attack on your town!" Daniel shouted.

"If that helps you pass the time, go right ahead," said Violet. "But you're not getting out of here for a very long time . . . and if you ever do, I promise you'll be a changed person."

Noah added, "A person learns a lot when his freedom is taken from him."

Daniel pondered that thought. He wanted to shout at Noah and Violet. He wanted to break free from the prison they had stuck him in, but there was no way out.

The gang left Daniel alone in the prison and walked into the town. Valentino the Butcher called out, "Is the town finally safe? Are the flying monsters gone?"

"Yes," Noah told Valentino. "It's time to rebuild."

The townspeople crowded around the group of friends. Violet announced, "Now that we have the jailhouse, we need to work together to keep a close eye on it. We don't want Daniel escaping."

Hannah added, "We also have to feed the prisoners and treat them fairly."

Valentino said, "If you can promise we are safe from those flying monsters and jumping cubes, I will serve them some food every day."

It was dusk, so the townspeople returned to their homes. Violet and Noah and their treasure-hunting friends headed to the tree house. Ben and Hannah wished them a good night and went to their house near the village.

"This is so cool," Lucy exclaimed as she climbed the ladder to the tree house.

Henry reached the top of the ladder and stepped into the living room. He liked to look out of the large window. "You can see the jungle from here!"

Max joined him at the window. "I think I can make out that arch in front of the jungle temple, too."

"I want to go back to the jungle temple," said Violet excitedly.

Noah was surprised. "I thought your treasure-hunting days were over."

Violet remembered the jungle temple and she imagined all the amazing treasure she might find in a chest there. "I think I'd like to go on a treasure hunt to that jungle temple. I just don't want to go back to the Nether."

"I don't want to go back to the Nether either," said Trent.

"Really?" Lucy couldn't believe it. "You don't want to find treasure in a Nether fortress?"

"Well, not for a while," replied Trent.

"I agree with him," said Will. "I'd go back to the Nether, but I don't want to go back any time soon."

The group sat at the table and plotted a treasure-hunting adventure to the jungle temple. They all got into their beds and went to sleep. Violet closed her eyes and dreamed of unearthing a big treasure chest in the jungle temple. She hoped they'd find diamonds inside.

16
OLD IDEAS

When she awoke in the morning, Violet gave her new treasure-hunter friends cake for breakfast and asked, "Are you ready for a treasure hunt?"

"Thanks," Lucy said as she took a bite of cake. "Yes, I'm definitely ready to go on an adventure."

"The jungle temple isn't too far away, and we will have enough time to head back and help the town rebuild after," remarked Noah.

The town had been severely damaged during the Nether mob attack and the gang needed to help rebuild it.

Violet said, "We won't be gone long. I have so many plans for rebuilding the village. I am going to help make this town better than it was before."

When the gang finished their cakes, they climbed down the ladder of the tree house and headed toward the jungle. The sun was shining and the sky was clear of hostile mobs. Everyone was hopeful they'd have a successful treasure hunt.

Noah stopped suddenly. "Wait! We can't leave without Hannah and Ben."

"Oh my gosh." Violet couldn't believe they had forgotten their friends. "I was so excited to go treasure hunting that I didn't even think about Hannah and Ben. That is awful."

"We all make mistakes." Lucy understood that Violet's excitement had made her forgetful.

The group knocked on Hannah and Ben's door. The two were ready for adventure—they wore armor and helmets, and carried pickaxes.

"We aren't going mining," joked Noah.

Henry said, "They're just being prepared. When you're a treasure hunter, you always have to be ready for an attack. I think you both are dressed appropriately."

The gang passed the village shopping area on their way out of town. Valentino the Butcher came out of his shop and asked, "Where are you all going?"

"We are finally going on a treasure hunt," Violet blurted out.

"When you come back with your treasure, make sure you stop by my shop, and I'll trade with you. I have some very good meat in stock."

The group promised to trade a portion of their treasure for meat. They would have a large feast once they returned, and then they'd start rebuilding the town.

After trekking through the grassy biome and passing fields of cows grazing peacefully, Max led the group down the sheared path toward the majestic jungle temple. Once they entered the temple, Max said, "We have to be very quiet. You never know what is in a jungle temple."

Violet immediately regretted that they didn't stop by the jailhouse to see if Daniel was still in his jail cell. Maybe he had escaped in the middle of the night and would stage another attack on them while they were in the jungle temple.

"Hannah," asked Violet, "did you happen to see if Daniel was still in his jail cell?"

"No." Hannah paused and said, "Ben, did you?"

Ben hadn't checked either and replied with another question: "Are you worried that he escaped?"

"Yes," admitted Violet.

"I thought somebody was in charge of watching Daniel. We have to trust that they're doing a good job," said Noah.

Violet decided that when they returned to town, she would devise a plan to warn the townspeople if Daniel escaped. She wondered if a siren might work. Although Violet was excited to be on the treasure hunt, she had this feeling that they could be attacked at any minute.

As the gang explored the three-story temple, Max stood on the moss stone floor and said, "We need to go to the bottom level to get the treasure. There is usually a trip wire. I can help us unearth the treasure without getting us destroyed."

Violet tried to ease her discomfort and said, "I'm so excited to see what we find. And I still can't believe we're finally on an adventure with Will and Trent and their treasure-hunting friends."

The group walked down the stairs. When they reached the bottom, Hannah called out, "Ouch! What was that?"

The gang searched for skeletons that might have spawned in the dimly lit temple basement, but, to their relief, there were no skeletons lurking around.

17
SHARING

Who's there?" Henry called out.

Noah grabbed his bow and arrow and readied himself to shoot the hidden attacker.

"Stop!" cried the voice. "It's me, Otto! I didn't realize I had hit Hannah. I thought you were treasure hunters who wanted to rob me."

Violet wondered if they should trust Otto. He had helped them end the Nether mob invasion, but he had also worked with Daniel. She asked Otto, "What are you doing here?"

"I am returning to my old treasure-hunting life. I left the town this morning." Otto stood by the levers where the treasure was hidden.

"Well, we aren't going to fight you, Otto," said Will. "We can all share the treasure."

But Otto didn't like that suggestion. "No. I got here first. This is my treasure."

"We're your friends!" exclaimed Violet.

Otto shouted, "Violet, you aren't a treasure hunter! That isn't how it works. In the world of treasure hunting everybody is working for himself."

Will defended Violet. "No, that's not true. Trent and I are a team, and we also work with Henry, Lucy, and Max."

"Well, I work alone, and I am claiming the rights to this treasure."

Lucy was upset with Otto. She had gone on other treasure-hunting adventures with him and they had always shared the treasure. "Otto, we have worked together and shared treasure in the past."

"After what happened with Daniel, I decided that I should work alone. I can't work with others."

Trent confessed, "I've also worked with Daniel. He is an evil person who forces you to become a bully. Now that you are free of him, you should be able to live the life you want. You shouldn't condemn yourself to a world without friends."

Otto paused, and then he walked over to the levers. He wanted to release the piston door, grab the treasure, and dash out with an inventory filled with diamonds or whatever might be in the chests. Instead, he said, "Maybe you're right. Maybe I should treasure hunt with you guys."

Violet didn't want to tell Otto that he made the right decision, so she just stood silently.

"Ouch!" Hannah called out again.

The group looked for other treasure hunters lurking around the jungle temple. Instead, they quickly spotted two skeletons at the end of the hall.

Otto aimed his bow and arrow at the skeletons and destroyed one. Hannah used her bow and arrow to obliterate the other skeleton. She walked over to the bones the skeletons dropped on the ground and asked Otto, "Do you want these bones for your inventory?"

"Thanks," Otto replied as he took the bones and placed them in his inventory.

Max offered his help to Otto. "I'm really good at unearthing treasure without having any explosions."

So, Otto let Max lead the dig for the treasure. Max carefully made sure not to activate the tripwires or to set off a TNT explosion. Max pulled out two large treasure chests. "Before I open these, I want to make sure that you're not going to attack us for the treasure, Otto."

Otto looked at the group of friends. "I promise. I will share the treasure with you. You are right—working together is better than working alone."

Violet gazed at the two treasure chests. She was overflowing with excitement. Part of her didn't want Max to open the treasure chest—she loved the idea of not knowing what they'd find. When Max finally opened the lid, Violet was glad he did.

"Emeralds!" Hannah called out. The green gems glowed.

Max handed out emeralds to everyone in the group. They each placed them in their inventory.

Henry opened the second chest.

Violet called out, "Diamonds!"

Then Noah cried, "Ouch!"

18
GREAT FINDS, GREAT FRIENDS

An arrow struck Noah as more skeletons spawned in the temple. The group aimed their bows and arrows at their target.

Max battled the skeletons and Otto joined him. Once the bony beasts were annihilated, Otto said, "I'd like to go on a treasure hunt with you, Max."

Max smiled and replied, "That would be fun. Let's go!"

The gang climbed up the stairs and exited the jungle temple. Violet, Noah, Hannah, and Ben were heading back to the village to help rebuild. Violet asked the treasure hunters, "Do you want to join us and come back to our village?"

Hannah added, "We'd like you to be a part of our town."

Lucy smiled. "Thanks. We've had that offer before, but we prefer to travel around the Overworld and search for treasure."

Max said, "If you ever want to join us on a treasure hunt, please do. We'd love to take you on another adventure."

Violet and her friends said goodbye to their new treasure-hunting friends. "Where are you headed now?" Violet asked.

Henry replied, "We're going back to the desert. We thought we saw a large temple when we were helping you rescue Will and Trent."

Will said, "I think there is a lot of treasure in that part of the desert. Also, I believe Daniel has buried treasure there."

"Sounds exciting!" exclaimed Hannah.

Will looked off in the direction of the village. "If Daniel ever escapes or stages another attack on your town, call us. We'll be happy to help you."

Violet and her friends thanked the treasure hunters and began their trip home. The sun was beginning to set, and they didn't want to get stuck battling hostile mobs.

It was dusk when they reached the town. Violet walked through the streets and inspected the damage. There was a lot to rebuild, but instead of being overwhelmed, she saw it as a fun challenge.

Valentino rushed toward them. "So, did you find any treasure?"

"Yes!" exclaimed Hannah, "We found emeralds and diamonds."

"Would you like to trade any of those precious gems for some meat?"

Violet didn't realize she was extremely hungry. She had used up most of her health bar during the treasure-hunting expedition. "I would," she volunteered and walked toward the butcher shop with Valentino.

"Before night sets in," said Noah, "we should have a big feast."

The group went to Valentino's butcher shop and exchanged a couple of gems for lots of beef.

When they exited the shop, Violet said, "I just want to check on something before we go home and eat."

Violet jogged over to the jailhouse. She peeked through Daniel's window. He appeared and asked, "Looking for me?"

"Yes, I was. I want to offer you some food," said Violet.

"Why are you being so nice?" Daniel sounded suspicious.

"I have a lot of good food and I thought I should give some to the less fortunate."

Hannah said, "But he doesn't deserve a good dinner."

When Violet handed Daniel the meat she said, "I hope you realize what you've done to this town and how much damage you've caused with all those attacks."

"I do," he grumbled and grabbed the meat through the small window in the cell.

The group walked away and began their feast. They had lots of celebrating to do before sunset. There were good reasons for their jovial celebration—they had finally trapped Daniel and they had inventories filled with treasure. And soon they'd have tummies filled with good food.

As the sun set, Violet and Noah climbed up the stairs to the tree house. Violet stood looking out at the dark sky. She was glad it was emptied of Nether mobs. Violet climbed into bed and thought about the amazing treasure-hunting adventure she had earlier that day before she drifted off to sleep.

DO YOU LIKE FICTION FOR MINECRAFTERS?

Check out other unofficial Minecrafter adventures from Sky Pony Press!

Invasion of the Overworld	Battle for the Nether	Confronting the Dragon	Trouble in Zombie-town
MARK CHEVERTON	MARK CHEVERTON	MARK CHEVERTON	MARK CHEVERTON

The Quest for the Diamond Sword	The Mystery of the Griefer's Mark	The Endermen Invasion	Treasure Hunters in Trouble
WINTER MORGAN	WINTER MORGAN	WINTER MORGAN	WINTER MORGAN

Available wherever books are sold!

LIKE OUR BOOKS FOR MINECRAFTERS?

Then check out other novels by Sky Pony Press.

Pack of Dorks
BETH VRABEL

Boys Camp: Zack's Story
CAMERON DOKEY,
CRAIG ORBACK

Boys Camp: Nate's Story
KITSON JAZYNKA,
CRAIG ORBACK

Letters from an Alien Schoolboy
R. L. ASQUITH

Just a Drop of Water
KERRY O'MALLEY
CERRA

Future Flash
KITA HELMETAG
MURDOCK

Sky Run
ALEX SHEARER

Mr. Big
CAROL AND MATT
DEMBICKI

Available wherever books are sold!